Some Things Are

SCA

WALKER BOOKS
AND SUBSIDIARIES
LONDON • BOSTON • SYDNEY

Florence Parry Heide

illustrated by Jules Feiffer

Getting hugged by someone you don't like

is scary.

Seeing something on your plate
you know you're not going to like

is scary.

Stepping on something
squishy when you're in
your bare feet

is scary.

Holding on to someone's hand
that isn't your mother's when
you thought it was

is scary.

Roller-skating downhill when you haven't learned how to stop

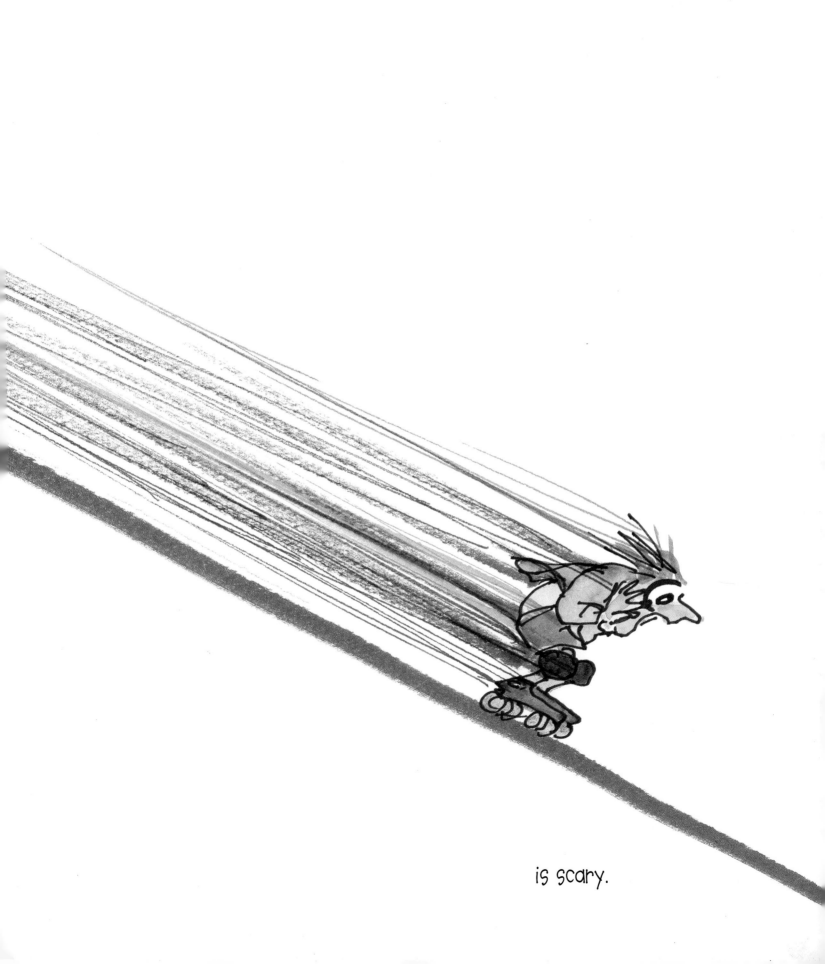

is scary.

Waiting to jump out and say BOO! at someone

Knowing that someone is waiting to jump out and say BOO! at you

is scary.

is scary.

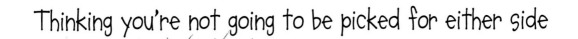

Thinking you're not going to be picked for either side

is scary.

Being on a swing when someone is pushing you too high

is scary.

Having an injection

is scary.

Telling a lie

is scary.

Stepping down from
something that is higher
than you thought it was

is scary.

Smelling a flower and finding
a bee was smelling it first

is scary.

Being with your mother when she can't remember
where she parked the car

is scary.

Discovering that your hamster cage is empty

is scary.

Getting scolded

is scary.

Finding out your best friend has a best friend who isn't you

Playing hide-and-seek when you're it and you can't find anyone

Having your best friend move away

is scary.

Thinking about a big bird with big teeth
who might swoop down and carry you away

is scary.

Brushing your teeth with something you
thought was toothpaste but it isn't

is scary.

Reaching under your bed for your shoes
and grabbing something—you don't
know what—

is scary.

Looking in the mirror while you're having a haircut and they're cutting it too short

is scary.

Thinking you're never going to get any taller than you are right now

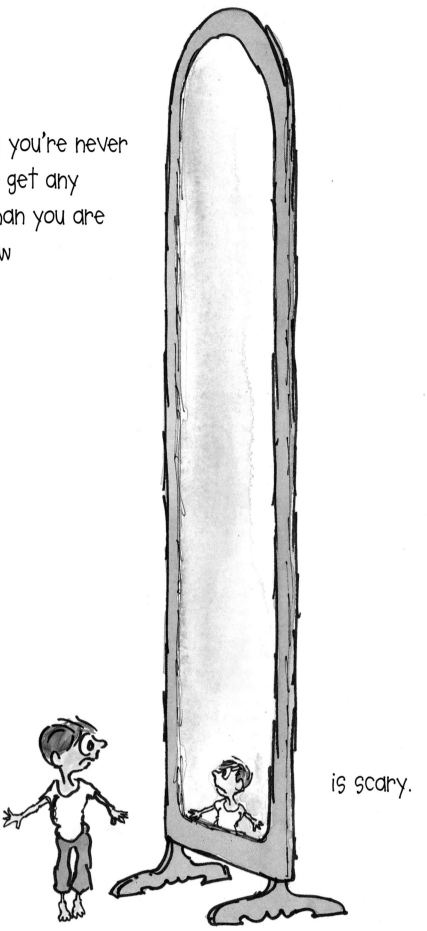

is scary.

Having to tell someone your name and they can't understand you and you have to spell it

is scary.

Knowing your parents are talking about you and you can't hear what they're saying

is scary.

Having people looking at you and laughing and you don't know why

is scary.

Climbing a tree
when you don't
remember how
to get down

is scary.

Being with your parents in an art museum and thinking you're never going to see the exit sign

is scary.

Knowing
you're going
to grow up
to be a
grown-up

is
scary.